CONTENTS

THE NIGHTMARE BEGINS

This morning, I was a normal kid. But by the end of the day, I'd become a hunted animal. And it was all because of Cindy Mackle.

The nightmare started on the way home from school. At the time, I didn't know it was the start of a nightmare. If I had, I would have got away from Cindy as fast as I could. But when someone asks you an ordinary question, you don't expect it to turn into a horror story or a nightmare – like when you're dreaming that you are running from a pack of lions, and your feet stick in the mud and the lions are getting closer and closer. What happened today was just like that. It gives me the shivers even thinking about it.

CHAPTER 1

I am walking home with Mungo and Scott, as usual. We are discussing things to do at our club when Cindy Mackle catches up with us.

Scott wiggles his eyebrows at Mungo and me. That's our secret sign to stop talking about the club. Then comes the question that starts the nightmare.

"Can I belong to your club?" Cindy Mackle asks.

The three of us sound like startled chickens.

"What club?"

"Whose club?"

"Huh!" (Mungo always says "Huh!" when he can't think of what to say.)

We all look at Cindy with horror, but she just puts her hands on her hips and laughs at us.

"You know! The club you have in the old shed at the bottom of your garden," says Cindy, turning her big brown eyes towards me.

I try to think of something to put her off the track. "The old shed? We've been cleaning it out."

"Yeah," adds Scott.

"What, after dark with torches?"

Cindy is smart and likes a laugh. She moved into the neighbourhood two weeks ago and she already knows most of what's happening, and what's already happened. She lives in the next street, but our yards back onto each other, with an old wooden fence between. She has the longest black hair I've ever seen. On her second day at school, she wore it out. It came down to her waist. She told the class she'd never had it cut. Totally amazing. It looked like a sheet of shiny black plastic.

"So...?" Cindy stares hard at us.

"Hang on," I say. "There are rules and things..."

"That's right! Rules!" follows Scott.

"Yeah! Rules!" echoes Mungo.

"What sort of rules?"

Mungo and Scott stare at me in total silence. We are left without a leg to stand on. We haven't got any rules for the club. Not one.

"Don't take too long deciding about your rules," Cindy says with a little smile on her face. "Otherwise, I might have to tell Mr Jenkins where his old rope is."

"We've only borrowed..."

"Shush, Scott!" I whisper.

Mr Jenkins lives next to Scott, at the end of the street. We borrowed his old rope for a swing-bridge between the two trees behind our club hut, but it didn't work. Now the rope is lying, like a dead snake, in the grass.

We move away from Cindy and start whispering.

"We can't let her join."

"But she knows about the rope."

"All we need is one rule. Something that would definitely stop her from being able to join."

"What's the problem?" teases Cindy. "Forgotten the rules?"

"She knows we haven't got any rules," says Scott desperately.

Then, just when everything is looking totally doomed, Mungo comes up with the most brilliant idea.

"How about the rule is..." Mungo says slowly, "you can't join unless you've got short hair."

I told you it was the most brilliant idea. It couldn't fail. There was no way Cindy would have her hair cut just so she could join our club. Sometimes Mungo has some stupid ideas, but this time... Wow!

"You tell her," he says to me.

We turn around and face Cindy.

"The first rule is that you have to have short hair."

"Short, short hair," adds in our Mungo, going overboard with his brilliant idea.

I expect Cindy to tell us it's not fair. Then I'll tell her that the second rule is that "no rules are allowed to be broken".

"OK," she says.

"But... but you've got long hair," I whimper.

Mungo and Scott look at me with pale faces.

"So... I'll get it cut."

"Short, short," says Mungo.

"What about your mother?" I ask.

Something is happening. Mungo's brilliant plan is turning a sickly green.

"It's *my* hair," says Cindy.

I don't know what to say. Is she having us on? Is she seeing how far she can play us? She must be. I decide to play her game. "OK. Get it cut and you can join our club!"

"What!" exclaims Scott.

"Huh!"

"No worries," I whisper, out of the side of my mouth. "She'll chicken out. You watch."

The next moment is the most awful one in my entire life. Cindy *doesn't chicken out.* Instead she says, "Which one of you is going to cut it?"

CHAPTER 2

Looking back now, I can see what Cindy was up to. She was waiting for us to chicken out. That was when I should have left it alone. I should have walked away and gone home to mow the grass or wash the dishes without being asked – even if it got Mum worried about me. Anything but hang around. But like a nightmare, once you're in it, it's hard to get out.

"You could draw straws to see who is going to be the lucky person to cut my hair," suggests Cindy.

The lucky person! I still can't believe she'll go through with it. Especially just to join our club! It'd be different if it was the Rockets. All we do is hang out in an old shed.

The three of us stand, like cardboard cut-outs, with open mouths.

Then Scott springs to life. "We haven't got any straws," he says.

"We could use bits of paper," suggests Mungo. Sometimes, I wonder whose side he's on.

Before Scott and I can protest, Cindy rips a page out of her exercise book. Then she tears the page into three different lengths.

"Close your eyes!" she orders.

When we open our eyes, the bits of ripped paper are sticking out from her clenched hand. They all look the same size.

"The person who pulls the shortest one gets to cut my hair."

None of us protest. It's like we're totally powerless.

"Who wants to go first?" asks Cindy with a grin.

"Mungo does," Scott and I say together.

"Huh?"

"Take one!" says Cindy. She holds out her hand. Mungo nervously shuffles his feet.

"Hurry up!" I yell. All this is starting to get on my nerves.

Mungo pulls out a long strip. He grins with relief.

"Next!" says Cindy.

Scott takes one. He pulls it out slowly, then waves it in my face. It's a long one as well.

Cindy uncurls her fingers. Lying in her palm is the last slip of paper. It is very short. And there is no doubt at all who the lucky one is – the one who is going to get to cut Cindy Mackle's long black hair.

CHAPTER 3

Before I can make an excuse, I find myself being herded down the street by Cindy.

"Now!" she says. "You can cut my hair now, while Mum's out."

I clear my throat. "But don't you like having long hair?" I know I sound like a wimp, but it's too bad. There's no way I want to be the one to cut Cindy's hair.

Cindy just laughs. "It's too heavy and it takes ages to wash and dry. I'm sick of it."

I'm not sure when Mungo and Scott actually disappeared, but one minute they were behind us, the next they had completely vanished.

This is when I made up rule number three: "In times of emergency, we stick together. No matter what! All deserters will be expelled from the club."

"You're not scared, are you?" says Cindy, leading me round to the back door of her house.

I shake my head. "No problem."

Before going into the house, I turn and look over the fence at our washing line. I can see Mum's blue jeans, two of my T-shirts and a whole lot of my little sister's clothes. At that moment, I'd give anything to be in my own backyard.

"Come on!" says Cindy.

I trail into the kitchen behind her. After dumping her backpack on the kitchen table, Cindy goes to the bread bin and takes out a packet of bread. "Want some?"

"Not hungry," I lie. How can she think of eating at a time like this?

I take off my backpack and wait. I keep hoping she'll tell me it's a joke.

Perhaps she'll say she's been having us on. Instead, she carefully butters the two slices of bread then spreads on a thick layer of peanut butter. She eats them very slowly.

When she's finished she goes and gets a pair of scissors. The long blades make a swishing sound as she opens and closes them.

CHAPTER 4

"Now remember, short. Real short," says Cindy, sitting herself down on a chair. If only Mungo hadn't added on the extra bit about her hair having to be real short, I might have been able to get away without cutting too much. Mungo the Bungo!

Even as Cindy undoes her hair and lets it spread over her back, like the night sky, and even as she hands me the scissors, I'm still waiting for her to shout, "Got you!" But she doesn't.

I take a handful of her hair and crunch into it with the scissors, and the nightmare hits me full force. It's worse than dreaming about a pack of angry lions and mountains of mud and stuck feet. I just want to wake up, but I can't wake up! I'm not asleep.

I just cannot believe this is actually happening. I'm really cutting Cindy Mackle's long hair.

Before long, most of Cindy's hair lies on the floor. It's like a deep, black puddle around my feet.

"What's it look like?" asks Cindy.

I gaze at her head. The hair that is left erupts in spikes and stalks.

Then, before I can reply, Mrs Mackle opens the back door.

After that, I don't know what happens. Someone screams. At first, I think it's me. But then I realize it's her. The scream is so awful, I nearly faint with fright.

CHAPTER 5

I don't know how I got out of Cindy Mackle's house alive.

By the time I arrive home, Mum is waiting for me. The nightmare is filling up with more and more "horrible people". Usually, Mum is nice. Usually, she smiles a lot and teases me. Usually... But today she starts yelling at me before I'm halfway in the house.

"What on earth possessed you..." After the first minute, I block out her ravings. Instead, I wonder what it would be like to be a uvula, stuck at the back of the throat – day after day – just hanging about. Except for times like this, when a uvula gets to do a lot of waving, I've never seen one so close before.

Now, thirty minutes later, I am holed up in my bedroom, just like a caged animal. No dinner! No television! And wouldn't you know it? Wednesday night is the best TV night of the week! Mum's told me to think about what I've done. I have, over and over. And I still reckon there was no way out. I still reckon it was Cindy's fault. I wish I'd never heard of her. I wish we never had a club...

A knock on my door interrupts my sad thoughts. I suppose it's time for another long lecture. But it isn't Mum. It's Cindy.

"It's OK," she says. "I told Mum that I made you cut my hair."

"Really?"

She nods. "Anyway I did, didn't I?"

I don't argue. The smell of bacon and chips cooking in the kitchen is driving me crazy. I need to eat! Then I laugh. Cindy's hair looks like it's been chewed. Worse than! It looks like it's been cut with an old, rusty lawnmower.

Cindy grins. "There was no way that Mum was ever going to let me get it cut," she says. "Now she can't do anything about it. Thanks, Amos."

I shrug.

"So, do we have a deal?"

A deal? What's she talking about?

"You know, that I can join your club," Cindy says.

I hesitate, then spit into my palm. Cindy does the same.

"OK. It's a deal," I say. We smack our hands together.

Later, when I'm sitting watching Max Million on my favourite TV show, I remember I haven't told Scott and Mungo the good news – about our newest club member. Too bad. There's no way I want to have two nightmares in the same day. One is more than enough! The next one can wait until tomorrow!

FROM THE AUTHOR

When we were children, my half-brother (I shall call him Timothy to protect his identity) always played with a little friend from down the road. One day, they found my mother's dressmaking scissors and decided to play "hairdressers". Timothy proceeded to cut off his friend's hair and then, as if this was not enough, he painted her skull with some old red paint from the garage. That was when the nightmare began – not only for Timothy, but for our mother, too.

Elizabeth Pulford

FROM THE ILLUSTRATOR

When I left school, I pursued a childhood ambition to work as an artist. In my first job, at a surplus supplies store, I drew hundreds of illustrations of clothing and boots. From there, I went on to illustrating comic strips and creating T-shirt designs. Today, I am doing what I love best: illustrating children's books. Sometimes, however, books present artists with nightmares, too. For example, what would you do, as an illustrator, with a plait, a boy, a pair of scissors and an empty cover page?

Richard Hoit

Written by **Elizabeth Pulford**
Illustrated by **Richard Hoit**
Edited by **Sue Ledington**
Designed by **Kristie Rogers**

© 1997 Shortland Publications Inc.
All rights reserved.

09 08 07
12 11 10 9 8

Published in Australia and New Zealand by MIMOSA/McGraw-Hill,
8 Yarra Street, Hawthorn, Victoria 3122, Australia
Published in the United Kingdom by Kingscourt/McGraw-Hill,
Shoppenhangers Road, Maidenhead, Berkshire SL6 2QL

Printed in China through Colorcraft Ltd., Hong Kong
ISBN 10: 0-7901-1649-9
ISBN 13: 978-0-7901-1649-5